P7-EGD-536

D0975767

The Talent Show

MICHELLE EDWARDS

Harcourt, Inc.

San Diego   New York   London

Requests for permission to make copies of any part of the work should be
mailed to the following address: Permissions Department,
Harcourt, Inc., 6277 Sea Harbor Drive, Orlando, Florida 32887-6777.

www.HarcourtBooks.com

Library of Congress Cataloging-in-Publication Data
Edwards, Michelle.
The talent show/Michelle Edwards.
p. cm.
"A Jackson friends book."
Summary: Second-grader Howardina Geraldina Paulina
Maxina Gardenia Smith is sure she will be the star of the talent show,
but when she gets up to sing at the dress rehearsal, she gets stage fright.
[1. Stage fright–Fiction. 2. Talent shows–Fiction. 3. Schools–Fiction.
4. Grandmothers–Fiction.] I. Title.
PZ7.E262Tal 2002
[Fic]—dc21 2001001227
ISBN 0-15-216403-0

First edition
A C E G H F D B
Manufactured in China

The illustrations in this book were done in pen-and-ink and
black-and-white gouache on Arches Hot Press watercolor paper.
The display type was set in Worcester Round Medium.
The text type was set in Sabon.
Jacket and case color separations by Bright Arts Ltd., Hong Kong
Manufactured by South China Printing Company, Ltd., China
This book was printed on Japanese matte paper.
Production supervision by Sandra Grebenar and Pascha Gerlinger
Designed by Lydia D'moch and Michelle Edwards

To Gioconda Sirolli and her dog, Lilly,
for their inspiring performance.

To Cindy Brush,
a wonderful bagpipe player,
Girl Scout troop leader,
and good-humored Scotswoman.

To Bridgett Stuckey and Earl Yowell,
with thanks for all their insight
on performance and stage fright.

And to the kids at
Horace Mann and Expo,
and talent show stars
everywhere.

Contents

# Howie

Howardina Geraldina Paulina Maxina Gardenia Smith jumped out of bed. Today was the day. Today was the Jackson Magnet Talent Show, and Howie was in it. So were her two best friends, Pa Lia Vang and Calliope James.

Howie brushed her teeth carefully. She used her special toothpaste with extra whiteners.

She smiled in the mirror. *Dazzling.*

She put a butterfly clippie in her hair. *Tah-dah*. She put in another one.

This morning Howie would sing in the Talent Show in front of the entire school. It was her last practice before Opening Night. Afterward there would be a big party with lots of yummy treats. Calliope's mom was baking fudge brownies. Pa Lia's grandma was making spring rolls. And Grandma Gardenia was bringing Howie's favorite, sweet potato pie.

Howie put on her shoes. She took a bow. She always remembered to bow at rehearsals. Some kids forgot. But Howie always remembered.

"When we bow, we are saying thank you to the audience," Mrs. Keyes would say. She was in charge of the Talent Show.

Tonight was Opening Night, the real Jackson Magnet Talent Show. Tonight, Howie would sing for the whole neighborhood. For the whole city. For the whole world. Tonight, Eric Hightower's mother was coming with the Channel Seven News Team.

Grandma Gardenia had almost finished making Howie's dress. It was special, with lots of sparkles. She would wear it tonight. Last night, Aunt Lilly had done Howie's nails.

Light pink and with a smidgen of shimmer.

Howie admired her nails. *Glamorous*, she thought. *Tonight, I will look glamorous.* The Channel Seven Nightly News, *starring*

Howardina Geraldina Paulina Maxina Gardenia Smith.

Howie bowed. *Thank you to my television audience.*

"Miss Howardina Geraldina Paulina Maxina Gardenia Smith, come downstairs right now, or you will miss your bus!" shouted Grandma Gardenia.

"Call me Howie," said Howie. She sashayed down the stairs. *A TV star needs a shorter name.*

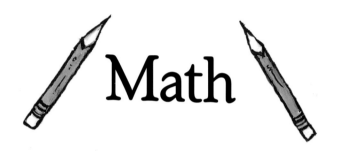

Math

"Twenty-five minutes to show time," said Calliope.

Howie felt warm inside. In twenty-five minutes, she would be on stage in front of the whole school. Singing.

"Are you ready?" asked Pa Lia.

"I've been ready for weeks," said Howie. "I'm so excited. I can hardly wait."

"Me, too," said Calliope. She and her dog, Woof, were going to perform tricks to music.

"I'm a little nervous," said Pa Lia. She was going to play the *thaj chij*. It was a musical instrument with two strings, made from coconut shell.

What's there to be nervous about? wondered Howie.

"Time for math," announced Mrs. Fennessey.

Howie wiggled in her seat. It didn't

seem fair to have math right before the Talent Show.

"Mrs. Fennessey, what about us kids in the show?" asked Stinky Stern, the enemy of the second grade. "Do we have to do math today?"

"Yes, but when you finish your work, you may put your papers on my desk and quietly leave the room. The rest of us will follow soon," said Mrs. Fennessey. She wrote lots of problems on the board.

Howie copied down the problems. She twirled her pencil. The numbers danced on the page. *Who can think about math now?*

Calliope gave Howie a gentle poke. "Finished. Meet you by the door."

Pa Lia tapped her on the shoulder. "Let's go. Calliope's waiting for us."

Howie quickly wrote down some numbers. She hoped they were right.

"Good luck," said Mrs. Fennessey.

Howie gave her a dazzling smile.

It was almost show time.

 # Almost

The whole school was gathered in the gym. Everyone sat on the floor. There were chairs for the parents who were helping with the party. The performers sat to the left of the stage.

Howie could see Grandma Gardenia. She was wearing a red dress with big white polka dots. And a rose.

Howie waved.

Grandma Gardenia smiled.

·Mr. Scott·

Mr. Scott, the principal, welcomed everyone to the Talent Show.

Howie quietly tapped her feet.

Then it was time to sing the Jackson Magnet school song. Howie sang her loudest.

The show began. The kindergartners were first. Catherine Rosenbaum sang "Twinkle, Twinkle, Little Star." Mohammed Parker played violin.

Squeaky but cute. Howie smoothed her dress.

Two first-grade girls twirled batons. Bridgett Thomas did a tap dance. Sabrina Stein recited a poem. She smiled the whole time and spoke really quietly. No one could hear her.

I will smile, too, but not when I'm singing. I want people to hear me, Howie thought.

Stinky Stern and his mom were next. They both played big bagpipes. They wore skirts and kneesocks. They were dressed like twins.

Howie put on some lip gloss. She didn't like Stinky Stern, but she loved the bagpipes. They filled the room with music.

17

Stinky and his mom bowed when they were done. Everyone clapped. A few kids hooted. Stinky stuck his tongue out at them.

Mrs. Keyes signaled to Howie. It was her turn.

# No Voice

Howie walked out on stage. Some-one's baby brother started to cry. There was some hushing and shush-ing, and then it was very quiet. Very, very quiet.

Howie looked out at all of Jackson Magnet. A gazillion heads were fac-ing her. And waiting.

Mrs. Keyes started to play Howie's music, "Simple Gifts."

Howie's heart was beating so loudly, she could barely hear the music. Her chest hurt. Her ears started ringing, and she thought she heard Stinky Stern laughing.

Howie opened her mouth, but the words wouldn't come out.

She had no voice.

The lights hurt her eyes.

Her feet were slippery in her shoes.

She couldn't move.

22

Mrs. Fennessey appeared. She rubbed Howie's back. "It's OK, Howie. Just sing."

But Howie couldn't sing.

Mrs. Fennessey motioned to Taniesha Yowell. She was a bossy sixth grader who sometimes baby-sat Howie. Taniesha stepped quickly across the stage and gave Howie a little poke. "Go, girl, go sing," she said.

But Howie couldn't sing.

Mrs. Fennessey nodded at Pa Lia and Calliope. They rushed up to Howie and took her hands. "Howie, we're here. We'll stay right with you. Just sing."

But Howie still couldn't sing. She

wasn't even sure she could breathe. Then she saw Grandma Gardenia floating toward her. She hugged Howie. It was a soft, pillowy, I-love-you hug.

"Home," said Grandma Gardenia.

The Ride

Howie was quiet on the way home. Quiet and cold. She and Grandma Gardenia had walked right off the stage and outside without their coats.

The big car was warm. The heater was buzzing and blowing. The windows were steamy. But Howie was still frozen.

Grandma Gardenia hummed and drove.

Howie wanted to say something, but she couldn't. She felt numb. She rubbed her hands together. *The Talent Show wasn't what I thought it would be.*

Howie closed her eyes. She tried to remember being on stage. She tried to remember what had made her so scared. But she couldn't.

Howie remembered Taniesha and Mrs. Fennessey talking to her. *What had they said?*

She remembered Pa Lia and Calliope holding her hands. Best friends. They had planned to be in the Talent Show together. Three stars from Room 201.

Now Howie didn't get to hear Pa Lia play or see Calliope and Woof do their tricks. No party afterward. No sweet potato pie. No best-friends stars.

Howie's leg twitched. *Stinky Stern.* He would laugh over this forever. Howie would be old and gray, like Grandma Gardenia, and Stinky Stern would tell her grandchildren about how she had messed up. How Howie couldn't sing. And how her grandma had to take her home from the Talent Show.

And what about Opening Night? What about her sparkly dress? What about the Channel Seven News Team's camera and the lights and all those people? Howie curled her toes. She blew on her freezing fingers.

The car stopped. Grandma Gardenia got out and opened the door for Howie. She gave her a huge hug.

They were home.

Home

Home. Howie took a deep breath. Home smelled like cookies and bread. And sweet potato pie. Too bad the pie was at school. At the Talent Show party. Howie chewed on her fingernail.

"I'm going to check on the bread," said Grandma Gardenia.

Howie walked slowly to the back door. She could hear pans rattling in the kitchen. She could see the dress Grandma Gardenia had made, hanging in the dining room. Her Talent Show dress. Finished.

Howie grabbed her dad's old parka. She slipped into Grandma Gardenia's warm furry boots. She put on her fuzzy mittens.

Howie headed outside. It was starting to snow. She found her place between the two oak trees. She saw Grandma Gardenia through the kitchen window.

"I'm Howardina Geraldina Paulina Maxina Gardenia Smith," said Howie very softly. It was good to hear her own voice again.

Howie started to sing:
   " 'Tis the gift
   to be simple.
   'Tis the gift
   to be free."

Howie sang just the way she had planned to sing in the Talent Show. Her voice was loud and strong. She used lots of expression. She even did some hand movements. And she remembered to bow.

"Terrific!" shouted Grandma Gardenia.

Howie looked at the back door. There was Grandma Gardenia, clapping.

Howie bowed again.

A squirrel raced in front of her.

Howie bowed to the squirrel.

A crow cawed on the fence.

Howie bowed to the crow.

She felt good. She felt great. She was the star of her backyard.

The Dress

Howie finished her piece of pie. Sweet potato pie. It had been on the table waiting when she came inside.

"I always try to bake an extra one for the family," said Grandma Gardenia.

Howie gave her a big kiss. Grandma Gardenia hadn't said one word about the Talent Show. She hadn't asked

Howie what happened. She hadn't even asked her about Opening Night.

Howie looked over at the sparkly dress hanging in the dining room.

"Should I try it on now?" she asked.

Grandma Gardenia smiled.

Howie took the dress up to her room. It smelled like vanilla and cinnamon and bread. Like Grandma Gardenia. And it fit perfectly. It was a star dress.

For tonight. Opening Night.

Howie grabbed her stuffed monkey and crawled into bed. She was cozy under the quilts. Safe and cozy.

She had to think about tonight. Grandma Gardenia would never make her go. Howie would have to decide for her-self.

Could she sing tonight with the Channel Seven News Team camera and a gazillion people watching her? Could she sing tonight like she sang in her backyard?

Howie hugged her little monkey. She got out of bed. She put some sparkly clippies in her hair.

I can do it.

Howie put on her socks with gold beads on the cuffs.

I can do it.

She stepped into her shiny black patent-leather shoes with the platform heels. She felt tall. Like a third or fourth grader.

Yes! I can do it. And if I get scared, I can close my eyes and pretend I'm singing in my own backyard. Or in my kitchen, with Grandma Gardenia.

Howie swirled and twirled and smiled her dazzling smile.

Opening Night

Howie's dad drove her to school. Pa Lia and Calliope were already there. Calliope's dog, Woof, licked her hand.

Pa Lia gave Howie a gold necklace with a special Hmong charm. "For good luck," she told Howie.

Calliope gave Howie a tiny plastic bag filled with gooey green stuff.

"I made it in science camp," said Calliope. "If you get nervous you can squish it around."

Best friends are great, thought Howie.

"It's the Three Muske-teers with their famous silent singer," said Stinky Stern. He was wearing a skirt again.

I don't care what Stinky says. Even if I was great, he'd make fun of me.

Howie sat down with her best friends. She watched the auditorium fill with people. She watched the Channel Seven News Team work

 their camera and lights. She watched the kindergartners and the first graders perform. She listened to Stinky and his mom play their bagpipes in their twin outfits.

Then it was her turn.

Howie walked on stage. She saw Pa Lia's mother, grandmother, and baby brother. They were all smiling at her. She saw Calliope's mom and dad. They were smiling at her. She saw her dad and Grandma Gardenia. They were smiling at her. She saw Taniesha Yowell.

She had her thumbs up. "You go, girl!" she mouthed.

Mrs. Keyes began Howie's music. Howie looked at Mrs. Keyes. She was smiling at Howie, too.

Howie smiled back at everyone.

"*'Tis the gift to be simple*," she began, " *'Tis the gift to be free.*"

Howie sang her song all the way through to the very end. She sang with lots of expression. The way she always sang at home. Then she bowed.

Thank you.

The whole auditorium clapped.

The Channel Seven News Team filmed every second of her song. They clapped, too. Howie hoped she would be on the evening news.

She was Howardina Geraldina Paulina Maxina Gardenia Smith.

She was a star.

 # Stage Fright

Howardina Geraldina Paulina Maxina Gardenia Smith is a star. But the first time she had her chance alone on stage, she couldn't sing. She couldn't move. She could barely breathe.

Howie had stage fright.

Lots and lots of people get stage fright—even stars. So what about the other kids in the Jackson Magnet Talent Show? Do you think they were scared, too?

Some kids get stage fright *before* they go on stage—like Pa Lia. But Pa Lia was used to being scared and nervous before performing. She often plays her *thaj chij* at Hmong festivals or for special occasions, like her grandma Ka Ghee's birthday.

Pa Lia's secret way to fight her stage fright is to practice. She practiced so much for the Talent Show, she didn't forget her music.

Calliope didn't even think about being nervous. When she performed, Woof was right there with her. And she had to make sure that Woof didn't get scared or bothered by all those people and bright lights.

If Stinky Stern was scared or nervous about anything, he'd never tell you. He'd just make fun of you, or trip you, or fake fart during your song. Then Stinky would feel happy, in a special Stinkster sort of way. Happy to stand on stage in a skirt. Happy to stand on stage with his mother. Happy to fill the Jackson Magnet gym with bagpipe music.

Talent shows can be great fun even if they are a little scary. So if there is going to be a talent show at your school or camp or rec center, you might want to try out. Do what you love to do best—read a poem, sing a song, dance a dance, perform tricks with your pet, or even play the bagpipes. Practice a lot. Have fun. And try not to be scared.

You can do it!

Pa Lia Vang

❁ has an older brother, Tou Ger
❁ loves to draw butterflies and mice
❁ is learning to turn cartwheels
❁ favorite food: noodles

Read more about Pa Lia in *Pa Lia's First Day:*

Pa Lia's first day at Jackson Magnet isn't going so well. She doesn't know anyone there. She can't find her second-grade classroom. But worst of all, she accidentally gets the only kids who have been nice to her in trouble. Will Pa Lia ever fit in?

Calliope Turnipseed James

❖ has one dog named Woof and zero grandparents
❖ loves to do math
❖ is learning to knit
❖ favorite food: Snickers

Read more about Calliope in
Zero Grandparents:

Mrs. Fennessey's class is planning a big celebration for Grandparents Day. Everyone is really excited—everyone except Calliope. Her best friends, Howie and Pa Lia, are bringing their grandmas. Even Stinky Stern's grandpa is coming. But Calliope doesn't have a grandma *or* a grandpa. How can she celebrate without a grandparent of her very own?

Howardina Geraldina Paulina Maxina Gardenia Smith

★ loves to sing
★ has a brand-new red ten-speed bike
★ is learning to use all the gears on her brand-new red ten-speed bike
★ favorite food: Grandma Gardenia's sweet potato pie

Read more about Howie in this book, *The Talent Show:*

Jackson Magnet is having a talent show. Howie is excited because everyone—mothers, fathers, grandparents, neighbors, teachers, kids, even the Channel Seven News Team—will be there to hear her sing. But at the final dress rehearsal, she gets scared and can't perform her song. How will Howie make it through Opening Night?

Matthew "Stinky" Stern

- has a pet parakeet named Petey
- loves being a stinker
- is learning to ride a two wheeler, with no hands
- favorite food: cowboy baked beans

Read more about Stinky in…
Hang on a minute. Does Stinky deserve a book?
You'll have to wait and see!